The
REBUS
TREASURY

Compiled by
Jean Marzollo

Illustrated and designed by
Carol Devine Carson

DIAL BOOKS FOR YOUNG READERS · NEW YORK

For Martine
J.M.

For Alex and all the Devines
C.C.

Acknowledgements and thanks to the following sources of rubber stamps: Leavenworth Jackson, 100 Proof Press, J. C. Casey, Bizarro, Mythology, Inkadinkado, and special thanks to Marty Blake.

Published by Dial Books for Young Readers
A Division of E. P. Dutton
A Division of New American Library
2 Park Avenue
New York, New York 10016

Published simultaneously in Canada by Fitzhenry & Whiteside, Toronto
Design by Carol Carson
Printed in Hong Kong by South China Printing Co.
First edition
COBE
10 9 8 7 6 5 4 3 2 1

Library of Congress Cataloging in Publication Data
Marzollo, Jean.
The rebus treasury.
Summary: Forty-one well-known songs and
nursery rhymes in rebus form.
1. Nursery rhymes. 2. Children's poetry. 3. Rebuses.
[1. Nursery rhymes. 2. Rebuses.] I. Carson, Carol
Devine. II. Title.
PZ8.3.M4194Re 1986   398'.8   85-16133
ISBN 0-8037-0254-X
ISBN 0-8037-0255-8 (lib. bdg.)

Table of Contents

Introduction

What is a rebus?
A rebus is a text in which pictures substitute for words, as in:

   U

I LOVE YOU

The rebuses in this book have been written for young children and their parents to sing and say together. A good way to go through *The Rebus Treasury* is for parents to run their finger under each line, pausing at the rebus picture and waiting for the child to "read" it. After a while the child will probably memorize most of the words to the songs and rhymes and will be able to read them on his or her own. Since rebuses are based upon the idea that symbols stand for words, they are an excellent introduction to the alphabet and reading.

Some of the rebuses used in this book are:

be   n o t   up   down   baby

dear   night   sheep   world

Part One

REBUS
RHYMES

I EAT MY PEAS
WITH HONEY

 eat my  with .

 've done it all my life.

It makes the  taste funny.

But it keeps them on my .

9

JACK AND JILL

 and went the

2 fetch a of .

 fell

And broke his

And  came tumbling after.

LITTLE BO-PEEP

Little  has lost her

And can't tell where 2 find them,

Leave them alone and they'll come ,

Dragging their behind them.

PATTY CAKE

Patty , patty ,

Baker's .

Bake me a

As fast as U .

Roll it and stretch it

And mark it with a B,

So we have

For 👶 and me.

MARY, MARY, QUITE CONTRARY

, quite contrary,

How does your  grow?

With cockle  and

And -slips all in a row.

LITTLE MISS MUFFET

Little sat on a tuffet

Eating her curds and whey.

Along came a

Who sat beside her

And frightened  away.

HEY, DIDDLE, DIDDLE

Hey, diddle diddle

The  and the

The jumped over the .

The little laughed

2 C such sport

And the ran away with the .

15

LITTLE BOY BLUE

Little

Come blow your .

The 's in the

The 's in the

But where is the

Who looks after the  ?

He's under the haycock

Fast  .

Will U wake him?

No,  .

4 if do

He'll surely

THE OLD WOMAN WHO LIVED IN A SHOE

There was an old

Who lived in a  .

She had so many

She didn't know what 2 do.

She gave them some broth

Without any  ,

Then said good-

And sent them 2  .

WEE WILLIE WINKIE

Wee  runs through the town,

👆 stairs and 👇 stairs

In his 👗.

Rapping at the 🪟,

🗣-ing through the 🔒.

R the 👶 in their 🛏s?

4 it's past 8 o-⏰.

DIDDLE, DIDDLE, DUMPLING

Diddle, diddle, dumpling, my son

Went 2  with his on,

1 off, the other on,

Diddle, diddle, dumpling, my son .

RIDE A COCK HORSE

Ride a cock 🐎 2 Banbury Cross

2 C a fine 👒 upon a ✏️ 🐎 .

With 💍 on her ✋ ,

And 🔔 on her 🦶 ,

She shall have music wherever she goes.

ONCE I SAW A LITTLE BIRD

Once  a little

Come hop, hop, hop;

So cried, "Little

Will U STOP STOP STOP ?"

 was going to the

2 say, "How do U do?"

But he shook his little

And far away he flew.

HICKORY, DICKORY, DOCK !

Hickory, dickory, dock,

The 🐭 ran 👆 the ⏰.

The ⏰ struck **1**,

The 🐭 ran 👇,

Hickory, dickory, dock !

OLD KING COLE

Old  was a merry old soul,

And a merry old soul was he;

He called for his

And he called for his

And he called for his fiddlers **3**.

Every fiddler had a

And a very fine  had he;

Tweedle **D**, tweedle **D**

Went the fiddlers **3**

And merry we will .

24

HUMPTY DUMPTY

sat on a   .

had a great fall.

All the   's

And all the   's

Couldn't put   together again.

25

IF ALL THE WORLD
WAS APPLE PIE

If all the 🌍 was 🍅 🥧,

And all the C was 🍾,

And all the 🌳 were 🍞 and 🧀,

What should we have 2 drink?

HICKETY, PICKETY, MY BLACK HEN

Hickety, pickety, my BLACK 🐔,

She lays 🥚🥚🥚 for gentle-👔 ;

Gentle-👔 come every day

To C what my BLACK 🐔 doth lay .

Sometimes 9 and sometimes 10 ,

Hickety, pickety, my BLACK 🐔 .

I ASKED MY MOTHER
FOR FIFTY CENTS

 asked my mother 4 50¢

2 C the 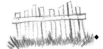 jump the .

He jumped so high

He reached the

And never came back

Till the 4th of .

Part Two

REBUS
SONGS

TWINKLE, TWINKLE, LITTLE STAR

Twinkle, twinkle, little ★,

How 👁 wonder what U R

☝ above the 🌍 so high,

Like a 💎 in the ✦.

Twinkle, twinkle, little ★,

How 👁 wonder what U R.

31

THE MUFFIN MAN

O, do U know the

The

The

O, do U know the

That lives on ?

O, yes know the

The

The

O, yes know the

That lives on  .

32

RING AROUND
A ROSY

 around a -y,

A full of .

Ashes, ashes,

All fall .

33

OH, DEAR! WHAT CAN THE MATTER BE?

O  what  the matter ?

, what  the matter ?

O  what  the matter ?

's so long at the fair.

He promised he'd buy me a

That would please me.

And then 4 a ,

0, he vowed he would tease me,

He promised 2 buy me a bunch of

2  my bonnie .

He promised 2 buy me a  of

A garland of , a garland of ,

A little straw 2 set off the

That my bonnie .

LAZY MARY

Lazy ![Mary] will U get ![finger]?

Will U get ![finger]?

Will U get ![finger]?

Lazy ![Mary] will U get ![finger]?

Will U get ![finger] 2 -day?

No, No, Mother,

 won't get

won't get

won't get

No, No, Mother,

 won't get

won't get 2-day.

OVER THE RIVER AND THROUGH THE WOODS

Over the 🕊 and through the 🌲

2 👵's 🏠 we go;

The 🐎 knows the way

2 carry the 🛷

Through the WHITE 🖍 and drifted ❄️.

Over the 〰 and through the 🌲

0 how the wind does 💨 !

It stings the 👃,

And bites the 🦶,

As over the 〰 we go.

38

EENTSY WEENTSY
SPIDER

The eentsy weentsy 🕷 went ☝ the 💦🔲.

🖐 came the ☁️🌧 and washed the 🕷 out.

Out came the ☀️ and dried ☝ all the 🌧.

And the eentsy weentsy 🕷

went ☝ the 🔲 again.

JINGLE BELLS

Dashing through the 🌨️

In a **1**-🐎 open 🛷

O'er the 🌲 we go

Laughing all the way

🔔 on bob-🧣 💍

Ma-👑 spirits bright,

What fun it is **2** ride and

A 🛷-ing song **2**-⬛.

O jingle  jingle

Jingle all the way,

O what fun it is 2 ride

In a 1-  open 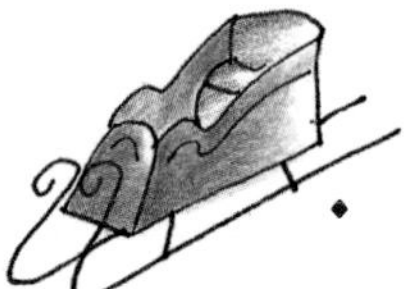 .

Jingle  jingle

Jingle all the way,

O what fun it is 2 ride

In a 1-  open 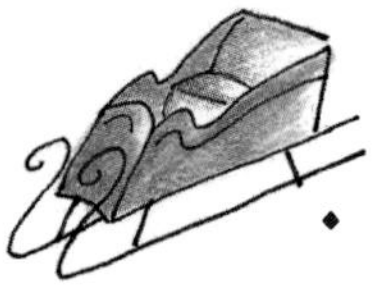 .

SHOO FLY

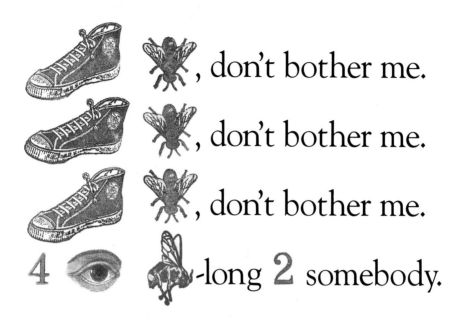

Shoo fly, don't bother me.
Shoo fly, don't bother me.
Shoo fly, don't bother me.
4 I belong 2 somebody.

I feel, I feel,
feel like a morning star.
I feel, I feel,
feel like a morning star.

POP! GOES THE WEASEL

All around the cobbler's

The chased the .

The thought 'twas all in fun,

goes the !

A 4 a of thread

A 4 a .

That's the way the goes

goes the !

43

HOME ON THE RANGE

O give me a 🏠 where the 🦬 roam,

Where the 🦌 and the 🐏 play;

Where seldom is heard a discouraging word,

And the ☀ is 🪢 ☁-y all day.

🏠, 🏠 on the range,

Where the 🦌 and the 🐏 play;

Where seldom is heard a discouraging word,

And the ☀ is 🪢 ☁-y all day.

RED RIVER VALLEY

From this valley they say U R going,

We will miss your bright 👁 👁 and sweet 👄,

4 they say U R taking the ☀-shine

That has brightened R pathways awhile.

Come and sit by my side, if U ❤ me.

Do 🪢 hasten 2 bid me adieu,

Just remember the 🖍 Valley,

And the 🤠 who ❤-d U so true.

DOWN IN THE VALLEY

 in the ___, the ___ so low,

Hang your ___ over, hear the wind ___,

Hear the wind ___, ___,

Hear the wind ___.

Hang your ___ over, hear the wind ___.

Build me a ___, 40 ___ high,

So ___ ___ C him, as he rides by.

As he rides by, by, as he rides by,

So ___ ___ C him, as he rides by.

Write me a ; send it by mail

Send it in care of Birmingham .

Birmingham , ; Birmingham .

Send it in care of Birmingham .

-shine, dew,

in heaven, know U.

Know U, U, know U,

in heaven, know U.

47

THE RIDDLE SONG

I gave my love a cherry that had no stone,
I gave my love a chicken that had no bone,
I gave my love a story that had no end,
I gave my love a baby with no cryin'.

How can there be a cherry without a stone?
How can there be a chicken without a bone?
How can there be a story without an end?
How can there be a baby with no cryin'?

A 🍒 when it's blooming, it has no 🌱,

A 🐓 when it's pippin', it has no ⫰,

The story that 👁 ♥ U , it has no end,

A 👶 when it's sleeping has no cryin'.

THE BEAR WENT OVER THE MOUNTAIN

The  went over the  ,

The 🐻 went over the 🏔 ,

The 🐻 went over the  ,

2 C what he could C .

2 C what he could C .

2 C what he could C .

The other side of the ,

The other side of the ,

The other side of the ,

Was all that he could C.

HUSH LITTLE BABY

Hush little 👶, don't say a word,

🎩 's gonna buy U a mocking 🐦.

If that mocking 🐦 don't sing,

🎩 's gonna buy U a diamond 💍.

If that diamond 💍 turns brass,

🎩 's gonna buy U a looking 🥛.

If that looking 🥛 gets broke,

🎩 's gonna buy U a billy 🐐.

If that billy 🐐 won't pull,

🎩 's gonna buy U a 🛒 and 🐂.

If that  and turn over,

's gonna buy U a named Rover.

If that named Rover won't bark,

's gonna buy U a and .

If that and fall

You'll still the sweetest little in town.

LAVENDER BLUE

Lavender's  , dilly dilly,

Lavender's ;

When am , dilly, dilly,

U shall a ;

Call your men, dilly, dilly,

Set them 2 work;

Some to the , dilly, dilly,

Some to the .

Some to make hay, dilly, dilly,

Some to thresh  .

While U and 👁, dilly, dilly,

Keep ourselves warm.

I'M A LITTLE TEAPOT

I'm a little ,

Short and stout;

Here is my ,

Here is my .

When get all steamed ,

Then shout:

Tip me over

And pour me out.

ROCK-A-BYE, BABY

Rock-a-bye,

On the   top.

When the wind   s

The   will rock.

When the bough breaks

The   will fall,

And   will come   ,

   and all.

OH, SUSANNA

come from ALABAMA

With my [banjo] on my [knee];

I'm going to LOUISIANA,

My true ♥ 4 2 C.

It [rain]-ed all [night] the day [eye] left,

The weather it was dry,

The [sun] so hot [eye] froze 2 death

SUSANNA don't U [cry].

O SUSANNA, O don't U [cry] 4 me.

[eye] come from ALABAMA with my [banjo] on my [knee].

58

had a dream the other ,

When everything was still.

 thought come

A-walking the ;

The  was in her 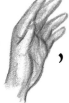,

The 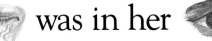 was in her ,

 said, " come from

 don't U  ."

BAA, BAA, BLACK SHEEP

Baa, Baa,

Have **U** any ?

Yes, sir, yes, sir,

3 full.

1 4 my master,

And 1 4 my dame,

And 1 4 the little

Who lives the lane.

Baa, Baa,

Have U any ?

Yes, sir, yes, sir,

3  full.

SING A SONG OF SIXPENCE

Sing a song of 6 pence,

A full of rye,

4 and 20

Baked in a  .

When the  was opened,

The  began to sing,

Wasn't that a dainty

2 set - 4 a ?

The  was in his counting ,

Counting out his 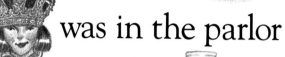.

The was in the parlor

Eating and .

The maid was in the 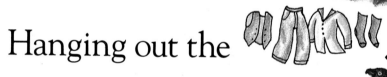,

Hanging out the .

Along came a

And nipped off her .

Using pictures to stand for spoken words is an ancient practice dating back to Egyptian hieroglyphs and early Chinese pictographs, which precede the alphabet. Rebus pictures were used to convey the names of towns on Greek and Roman coins and on family seals in Europe. Later they evolved to rebus riddles, as we know them today.

The artwork in *The Rebus Treasury* is comprised of rubber stamp images and original colored pencil drawings. The stamp art is taken from nineteenth century engravings and twentieth century line drawings.